Stories by Fatimah

Stories by Fatimah

A Collection of Short Stories by:
Fatimah Soltanian Fard Jahromi

Soltanian Publications

This edition first published in 2021

Published by Soltanian Publications, Auckland

The inside illustrations by Fatimah Soltanian Fard Jahromi

ISBN 978-0-473-57932-6 (paperback)
ISBN 978-0-473-57933-3 (kindle)

A catalogue record for this book is available from the National Library of New Zealand

Contents

1
Tiny Spaceship

Tiny Spaceship

Victoria was sitting at home playing video games. It was a stormy night. Her parents were away on a business trip. Victoria's grandmother was taking care of her while her parents were away. But her grandmother had fallen asleep and Victoria was still on her computer. Victoria turned off her computer and decided to go to bed. She made her bed and kept trying to fall asleep but she kept hearing noises. She didn't know what it was or where it was coming from. "What is that noise?" said Victoria to herself.

She looked out her window to see what it was. She could not believe what she was seeing. It was a tiny little spaceship. She watched as it landed. The spaceship's door began to open but she didn't see anything coming out of it. "Grandma! Wake up," said Victoria.

"What is it?" said Victoria's grandmother.

"I see a spaceship."

"You have been playing too many video games," said her grandmother. "Go back to sleep."

Victoria's grandmother fell right back to sleep. "But it is right there," said Victoria.

Victoria got out her phone and took a picture of the little spaceship. "I can't take a proper picture through this window," uttered Victoria to herself. "But I can't go outside."

Victoria put her phone down and got out her remote control toy and maneuvered it to fly out the window. Victoria controlled it in a way so it could grab the little spaceship. Using the remote control toy, Victoria successfully grabbed the spaceship and brought the little spaceship into her room through the window. "Yes, I got it!" said Victoria with excitement. "Now to show Grandma."

"Grandma, look!" Victoria tried waking her grandmother up again but she was so fast asleep that she wouldn't wake up. Victoria started to shake her.

"Stop it, go to sleep," said her grandmother.

"But look! It's the spaceship," said Victoria.

"Don't play with your toys now, you need to sleep," said Victoria's grandmother.

Victoria's grandmother fell back to sleep again. Victoria started to look at the little spaceship.

"I wonder how this works," said Victoria. "I should study it to figure out how it works. Maybe it has lasers and little aliens inside it."

Victoria tried to look inside the spaceship but because it was so tiny it was hard to see what was inside. So she tried to focus more. Victoria saw little controls inside. Victoria then saw the door closing. "Oh no!" said Victoria. "It's going to fly away."

Victoria put a glass cup over the spaceship so it doesn't fly away. The ship tried to fly away but couldn't. The little ship's door opened again. Victoria heard little squeaky noises and saw the little controls moving. "Wow, the aliens must be really tiny," said Victoria. "Hi, little guys. Is anyone in there?"

Victoria then saw them move more controls and heard them talking in a different language. "Wow, you guys have a machine that makes you louder?" said Victoria. "That's so cool but I can't understand you."

Victoria saw more controls moving and they kept speaking in different ways. It seemed like they were tweaking their machine to recognize Victoria's language. "Are you guys trying to find my language?" asked Victoria.

The aliens finally started speaking English and then started talking to Victoria. They had found her language using their translating machine.

Each one of the aliens started turning off their invisibility cloaks. Victoria saw tiny furry creatures controlling the spaceship, similar to cute bunnies. "Let us go. Our ship was damaged and we were stuck on this planet. We've repaired our ship and we need to get off this giant planet with giant creatures," said one of the aliens.

"I want to learn about you and your machines," responded Victoria.

"This is one of the children of the humans, remember what we observed?" said one of the other aliens that looked like a scientist.

"But you can't keep us caged because you want to learn about us," said the alien leader.

Victoria realized her mistake of holding the aliens against their will and that she was being cruel to the aliens through her actions. She removed the glass cup and apologized.

The aliens and Victoria spent the whole night talking and they became good friends. Just before sunrise the aliens said they had to go home but they promised Victoria that when she is a bit older and able to understand things better they will return and teach her about their technology.

Just before sunrise the aliens left. Victoria ran to her grandmother, "Grandma, grandma! You won't believe what just happened."

Victoria told her grandmother what had happened during the night. Victoria's grandmother smiled and said to her, "Oh Victoria. You have such a wild imagination. It was probably just a dream."

But Victoria knew she hadn't slept yet.

2
The Roller Coaster Ride

The Roller Coaster Ride

Luke had just woken up from a long sleep. Luke was bored so he decided to wake his sister up. Luke ran into his sister's room and put his toy beetle on his sister's face. "Wake up Joy there's a beetle on your face," said Luke.

"A beetle!" shouted Joy jumping out of her bed. She threw the toy beetle off of her face and started stepping on it.

"Hey wait that's my toy beetle," said Luke.

"Your toy! Will you stop playing pranks on me all the time," said Joy.

"Fine this might be the last one," said Luke nefariously.

Luke and Joy brushed their teeth and ate breakfast. After they finished eating they went to the yard to play on the swings. When they were playing they heard their father talking on the phone and he sounded excited. Their father was an engineer and he worked at the Coney Island amusement park next to the beach. "Let's go ask Dad what he is so excited about," said Luke.

"Yes, let's go," said Joy.

Luke and Joy got off the swing and started to run into the house. They asked their father what was going on and what he was so excited about. "What are you excited about?" asked Luke and Joy.

"The roller coaster is complete and I am going to go and test it out," said their father.

"Can we go on it too?" asked Luke.

"No, it's a test run, we have to test its safety, but you can come along and watch," said their father.

Luke and Joy got excited as well and they started jumping up and down. Luke and Joy ran to their room to get ready to go.

After everyone got dressed they all hopped into the car and drove to the amusement park. When they arrived at the amusement park they saw the roller coaster and it was huge. It was 50 meters high.

"This is so awesome! It is way higher than before," said Joy.

"Are you going on the roller coaster now to test it?" said Luke.

"Yes Luke, I am," replied their father.

Their father went on the roller coaster. The roller coaster started its slow ascent to the top. It was getting ready to go back down. The roller coaster was about to go down but then it suddenly stopped and wasn't moving anymore. "Hey Luke, do you see the rollercoaster moving?" said Joy.

"Oh no! It must be stuck," shouted their father from the top of the roller coaster.

"This is not good," said Luke with a worried face.

The rollercoaster operator kept trying to get him down but it wasn't working. "Can't he just climb down?" said Luke.

"No, it's too dangerous," said the operator.

Instead of moving him forward the operator tried to bring him back but that wasn't working either. He tried using different controls to no avail.

"None of these controls are working," said Joy.

"Yes, I noticed that," said the operator. The controller got out his phone and started making calls about the situation. He called another engineer to get advice on what to do about the rollercoaster. "Ok, I called for help," said the operator.

"Good, now we just have to wait for her," said Luke. "Is she going to be coming in two or three minutes?"

"Probably a little longer than that," said the operator.

After a while the engineer arrived. She started looking at the roller coaster to see what went wrong with it and if they could find the problem and the solution.

"This is going to take a while isn't it Luke?" asked Joy.

"Yes, it is," replied Luke.

After a while the engineer still hadn't done anything with the roller coaster to get the father down.

"While you figure out the problem I will just call a rescue helicopter to get him down from there," said the operator.

The operator called a rescue helicopter. It had been half an hour and the helicopter still had not arrived. When they were waiting the operator's phone alarm turned on.

"I didn't set my alarm" said the operator.

The operator looked at his phone and it was sounding a warning alert siren about a tsunami which was about to hit the beach near them.

"What! How many bad things can happen in one day," said Luke.

"Where is that rescue team!" shouted their father.

They all got worried and their father didn't want Luke and Joy getting hurt.

"Operator, get the kids out of here," said their father.

"Yes sir," said the operator.

"But Dad what about you?" asked Luke.

"Yeah, we're not leaving without you," said Joy.

"Hurry Smith, put them in your car," said their father.

The operator picked both of them up and put them into the car and drove away. The engineer also left with them. Their father started to climb down the roller coaster. He climbed as fast as he could and hoped that he could make it. The tsunami was coming right for them but just then a rescue helicopter threw down a rope and told him to climb.

"It's about time you guys got here," said the father while climbing into the helicopter.

He got in and they started to fly away as fast as they could. The helicopter was getting a little out of control. It was twisting and turning. But eventually the helicopter flew away and the tsunami never made it to the amusement park. Everyone was safe. After that the father immediately called the operator to see if the kids were alright.

"Don't worry they're safe," said the operator.

"Thanks for getting them out of danger Smith," said the father.

"I'm sure you would have done the same for my kids," replied the operator.

The kids and the operator drove to the father. The kids ran out and gave their father a big hug. They all hopped into the car and went back to their home.

3
The Walking Stick

The Walking Stick

There once was a panhandler called Alexander who would play drums on the street corner to earn money for a living. Alexander walked with a limp. Jason, a businessman, lived on the same street as Alexander. Every time he passed Alexander on the street he would mock Alexander for his limp. Jason wouldn't give Alexander any money whenever he played the drums and would always act annoyed when passing Alexander. Alexander didn't like Jason's behavior towards him but he chose just to ignore him.

One day Jason was walking by Alexander again but this time he stopped by the market to buy some new clothes. Jason bought his usual fancy clothes. When Jason was shopping he saw a woman selling walking sticks. He saw a very fancy looking walking stick with a gold coloured handle and wanted to use it as a fashion accessary for when he goes out at night. Jason asked the stick seller to see the fancy walking stick. The woman showed it to him and it looked very elegant. The woman explained that the walking stick may look beautiful but it has a chip at the bottom and it can't be used as a walking stick. "If you want to buy this I must warn you that it doesn't work well," said the stick seller.

An evil thought came into Jason's mind. He thought to himself, "I'll buy this walking stick and give it to Alexander as a peace offering. Then when he uses it and realizes it doesn't work I'll mock him."

"Don't worry this is exactly what I need," said Jason to the stick seller.

"Ok, but you can't ask for a refund later," said the woman.

Jason went out of the market and walked towards Alexander and told him "I have a gift for you."

"This is one of my best ideas," thought Jason to himself. "He will feel so shameful when he thinks he doesn't know how to use it." Jason walked to Alexander and said that he has a gift for him.

"Why would you get me a gift?" asked Alexander.

"I realized my mistake," said Jason suspiciously.

Jason got the walking stick out of the bag and told him that this gift will help him walk better.

"Thank you so much. This is a very kind and thoughtful gift," said Alexander.

"Yes, I am so glad you like it," said Jason walking away with a smirk.

The next day Jason went to see if Alexander was having trouble with the chipped walking stick. But Jason was surprised by what he was seeing. Alexander was using the walking stick perfectly without any difficulty. "What! How is he walking with that walking stick when it's chipped at the bottom?" said Jason to himself.

Jason got furious and he went to the woman selling walking sticks to see how he was walking. "How is he walking with that stick?" asked Jason.

"You mean the fancy one I sold you?" asked the woman.

"Yes! That one," said Jason.

"I'm sorry, but I don't know. He shouldn't be able to," said the woman.

Jason left the market in anger. He went up to Alexander and said that he wanted it back. "Why do you want it back?" asked Alexander. "You gave it to me as a gift."

"Well, I want it back. I gave it to you, so I can take it back if I want to," said Jason.

Alexander gave back the walking stick to Jason. Jason decided to use the walking stick as a fashion accessory to go with the new clothes he bought that night when he was going out to a party. Jason was very excited to try it out but every time he walked he kept tripping. He didn't know how Alexander could walk so nicely but he wasn't able to do the same. Jason got even angrier and went back to the woman who sold it to ask for a refund. He banged the table and started complaining about how he wanted a refund. "You can't have a refund for this item, I already warned you it doesn't work," said the woman.

"What on earth am I supposed to do with it?" yelled Jason.

"You could go ask that other man how he was using it so well," said the stick seller mockingly.

Jason stormed out of the market again and ran to Alexander. He demanded to know how he walked with it. "Tell me how you did it? Here show me," demanded Jason angrily.

"But you took it from me and now you want to give it back again," said Alexander.

"Ok I promise I won't take it back again if you show me how you did it," said Jason.

Alexander made Jason to keep his word once he shows him how he used the walking stick.

"When you first gave this to me I saw the chip at the bottom," said Alexander.

"Wait, you saw it?" said Jason surprisingly.

"Of course I did, it is a very obvious chip," said Alexander.

"Well, I didn't think that you would notice," said Jason.

"I did. Now listen very carefully," said Alexander.

Alexander told him that after noticing the chip he figured out a specific way of walking with it so that it can work properly as a walking stick. "You just have to use it in a way that you don't lean on the chip."

Jason felt so embarrassed and couldn't say a word. Then Alexander taught Jason an important lesson in life.

Alexander said, "Sometimes it's not about the walking stick but the person that uses it."

Jason walked away and after that he didn't bother Alexander anymore.

4
Jane's Kitten

Jane's Kitten

Jane had just finished getting ready for high school. She walked out of the house and started walking to school. Jane didn't have any friends at school or any siblings so she would spend most of her time alone. She walked to school alone and studied on her own. She wasn't a talkative person either but always loved to talk to animals and make friends with them. Her mother was a vet so Jane could see adorable animals all the time but she didn't have her own pet. She had always wanted one.

One day when Jane was walking to school she heard a purr. She went to see where it was coming from. Jane saw that the noise was coming from a garbage bin. She opened the garbage bin and saw a little kitten inside. It looked adorable. Jane picked up the kitten and got it out of the garbage bin. She saw that the kitten's leg was broken. "Don't worry little kitten, I can take you to my mum, she'll help you," said Jane.

After Jane finished her school for the day she took the little kitten to her mum. Jane's mother wrapped the little kitten's leg up with a cast. "This will do it for now but it will need to heal so don't take off the cast," said her mother.

"Can we keep him, please?" asked Jane.

"You can keep him but you have to make sure to take good care of him," replied her mother.

Jane got ecstatic and she promised to take good care of the little kitten. She always took the little kitten everywhere she went and spent a lot of time with him. One day Jane thought since she had been spending so much time with the kitten she was going to give it a name and not call it kitten anymore. She decided to name him Lion because she thought he was a brave kitten.

One day when Jane was walking to school she bought a collar for the kitten and wrote Lion on it. When she got back home she was excited to put it on the kitten. Her kitten ran to her and he seemed really happy.

"What are you so excited about?" asked Jane.

Jane saw that Lion's leg was back to normal.

"Yay, your leg is back to normal!" said Jane.

Later that day Jane went to sleep and she put Lion in his little bed. When she woke up she saw that the kitten wasn't there. She got worried because Lion would never leave his bed without jumping around and making noise. She checked all around the house and in the yard but Lion was nowhere to be seen. "Oh no, I've lost him!" said Jane.

Jane went back and forward to different places. She went to her school, the park and the shop. Jane decided to tell her mum what had happened. "Don't worry Jane, I'm sure he will come back to you," said her mother.

It was night time and Lion still wasn't back. She couldn't sleep through the night because she kept thinking about him. She thought that he might be hurt or lost. When she woke up and walked to school she hoped to see her little kitten, but Lion wasn't there.

She remembered all the times they spent together and she started to miss him. She tried finding another kitten but it wasn't the same. "What am I going to do?" said Jane. She started to put up posters of her missing kitten and going to people's houses to ask if they had seen it but nobody had.

While putting up posters with her mother, Jane heard a purr and thought that it might be her kitten. She ran to see where it came from. She had to go into a dark alley if she was going to find out what it was that was making the noise. She wanted to go in but she didn't know if she should. Jane went to her mother and asked if they could check in the alley to see if her cat was there. "I think Lion is in that Alley," said Jane.

"Well, we can take a look but I don't think it's the same kitten," replied her mother.

Jane and her mother went into the dark alley. As they went forward, the purr started to get louder. "It's coming from that garbage bin," said Jane.

Jane opened the garbage bin but nothing was there. She started digging through the garbage to see if Lion was underneath all the rubbish. Then she heard a purr coming from inside a garbage bag. She opened up the garbage bag. Jane saw her little kitten Lion. "How can you tell this is your kitten?" asked her mother.

"It has the same collar," said Jane.

But it wasn't just Lion hiding in the bag. Lion's siblings were also there with him. Three cats came out from behind the garbage bin and they looked exactly like Lion. "That's why you were gone for so long, you were with your brothers and sisters," said Jane.

Jane decided to take them all home and take care of all of them. She named Lion's sisters Coco and Sunshine, and Lion's brother was called Sylvester.

5
Small but Big Problems

Small but Big Problems

Jake, Sarah and Diego were three friends. These three friends were all scientists and shared one lab for their research. They were working on a chemical to decrease the size of any object. One day they managed to complete the chemical and began the testing phase. They decided to test the chemical on one of their lab mice. They poured the chemical onto a mouse and it worked. The mouse shrunk to a very small size. But then they realized there was one problem. They hadn't found a way to reverse the effect if they needed to. They went to work on finding a solution to reverse the effect.

One night the three scientists were working late in the lab and Diego felt tired and said that he wanted to go home. "I'm really tired, I'm going home," said Diego.

"Ok, see you later," said Jake and Sarah.

When Diego was exiting the room, as he shook hands with Jake, they accidently knocked one of the test tubes off the table and the chemicals splattered everywhere. It went all over Diego, Jake, and Sarah. They all started shrinking until they were as tiny as ants. "Look at what your clumsiness has done!" said Sarah.

"It's not our fault, you shouldn't have left it there!" shouted Jake.

"You're the one who put it there!" shouted Sarah.

"Well, you should have moved it," said Jake.

"Hey, we shouldn't fight, we need to work together to fix this," said Diego.

"Fine, but afterwards I am having a talk with Jake," said Sarah.

"And I'm going to have a talk with Sarah," said Jake.

They all started thinking of a plan. Sarah and Jake were still fighting during that time and Diego had to keep calming them down. Later, when they were thinking about a solution Diego got an idea. "I have an idea, we can ask my dad for help," said Diego.

"Why your dad?" asked Sarah.

"Because he is a scientist but he has retired now," said Diego.

"It's a good thing the door is open otherwise we wouldn't be able to reach the door knob," said Diego.

They all left the lab and while they were walking to the house they had to make sure not to get stepped on by other people. It was taking a while to get there since they couldn't use their car due to their size. It took them an entire week. They had to scavenge for food and water on their way to Diego's dad's house.

During the trip, they had to work together to maneuver the difficulties they were facing. The friends finally made it to Diego's dad's house. They tried knocking but they couldn't do it hard enough for Diego's dad to hear them.

"What do we do now?" asked Sarah.

"We need to find another way in there," said Jake.

When they were looking for a way to get in, the door opened and Diego's dad walked out. They all tried calling him but he couldn't hear anything because they were so tiny. At one point Diego's dad almost stepped on all three of them.

Diego decided to go on his dad's toe so that his dad would think there is something on his toes and look down and see the three of them. At first Diego's dad thought it was an ant and almost threw Diego off his foot. But then he looked more closely and saw that it was Diego but really tiny. "Diego is that you?" asked Diego's dad.

He brought Diego close to his ears so he could hear them. Diego shouted for his dad to hear him. "We were making chemicals and now it made us tiny and we need you to help us go back to normal," shouted Diego.

"Why are you shouting?" asked Diego's dad.

"I thought you can't hear me," said Diego.

"You should have been more careful, I might not be able to fix this," said Diego's dad.

Diego's dad took all three of them to the lab to find a cure. He started mixing chemicals and testing them on the mice. It was taking days. "Ever since you were a kid I had to help you from all those crazy experiments you did," said Diego's dad.

"I just really liked experiments Dad," said Diego.

"You take after me," said Diego's dad.

Diego's dad told the three friends that he needed to go out and get some more ingredients to prepare the solution and that they had to stay in the lab until he got back. So, they all waited for him to get back. Jake was getting a little bored. "Hey you guys want to play twenty questions?" asked Jake.

"Not now Jake I'm trying to think about how to fix us, you should too," said Sarah.

Diego sighed and also tried to think of a remedy. When they were waiting, the lab cleaner came in with water and a broom. He was coming towards them. "Make sure not to get hit by that broom," said Jake.

They were running in circles away from the broom and water until they finally started to climb up a small chair. It was a bit hard since they were tiny. They got up there and waited for the cleaner to finish his work.

The cleaner later left and they all managed to stay safe. Diego's dad returned and he said that he couldn't find one of the ingredients to completely finish the solution. If they didn't have that specific chemical they would be ten centimeters or about four inches less than what they already are. "I'm already short and now I have to be shorter!" shouted Sarah.

"I could make the ingredient but that would take at least two more weeks," said Diego's dad.

"You got to do it?" pleaded Jake.

Diego's dad agreed to do it. He spent two weeks making the ingredient for the solution. Then he spent two more days mixing those ingredients together in the right order and the right way. "I've almost finished it," said Diego's dad with excitement.

"Yes!" shouted Diego.

Jake was jumping up and down on the table and he knocked over one of the chemicals they needed to complete the main solution. "Oh no," said Jake.

"What is wrong with you? Haven't you learned your lesson?!" shouted Sarah.

"At least this isn't the one I had to make but I have to go and get it again," said Diego's dad.

Diego's dad came back with the ingredient and started to mix it. He had to make sure to add exactly three drops of it or the solution wouldn't work. He completed the chemical and poured the solution on all three of them. They started to quickly grow back to the height they were. "Thanks Dad for helping us out," said Diego.

"Your welcome but just be more careful next time," said Diego's dad.

"Okay, we will," replied Diego.

"Mostly Jake needs to be more careful," said Sarah.

They all laughed together and went back home.

6
The Portal

The Portal

Tara and David were siblings and had just returned from school. Tara was twelve and David was six years old. "That was a long day at school," said Tara.

"Yeah, I'm going to go play now," said David.

"Ok, I'll come in a minute," said Tara.

When Tara got home she decided to pick out her outfit for the next day. She opened her closet and pulled out one of her shirts. As Tara removed the shirt from the closet, she saw something in there. It was golden and glowing and it started to get bigger. It looked like it was a portal. The portal started to suck the clothes in and Tara almost got pulled in too. "What on earth is going on?" said Tara. She held on to the wall so she wouldn't get sucked in.

The portal was getting out of control. While holding on, Tara saw her room's door opening. David walked in to see what was going on. He came inside and also saw the portal. The portal also started to pull in David. "What's going on?" asked David.

"Hold on to something!" yelled Tara.

"Ok," said David worryingly. David tried to hold on to something but he couldn't do it fast enough and he got sucked in. The portal closed just before Tara could jump in. David was gone. "Nooo!" shouted Tara.

Tara's parents heard Tara shout and they went to see what was going on. She started explaining what had happened. "Mom, Dad something horrible has happened, David just got sucked into a portal!" said Tara in a worried way.

"What!" shouted Tara's mother.

"Tell us everything, where was the portal?" asked Tara's father.

Tara brought her parents to her closet and told them, "David got sucked in through there."

"He got sucked into the portal and I tried to save him but the portal closed," said Tara.

Tara's father looked in the closet and didn't see anything. Tara also looked in the closet and saw soil. "What's this soil doing here?" asked Tara.

"Maybe the soil came from the portal," said Tara's mother.

They spent all night thinking of where David could be and how they could get him back. While they were still trying to think of a way to get him back, Tara fell asleep.

Tara's mother went to get coffee to stay awake. When she left, the portal opened again. Tara woke up. "It's the portal, it opened again," said Tara. It did the same thing. It first opened and got bigger. The portal started sucking things in again. Tara and her father tried holding on but this time it was stronger. Their fingers slipped off the wall. The portal pulled them in and it closed up. Tara and her father fell through. They saw that they had fallen in a place that seemed to be underground.

"We have to find David and then find a way to get back," said Tara's father. Tara and her father went looking for David. They walked and walked.

"How far do you think David might have gone?" asked Tara. After walking for a while they saw an underground village. "An underground village," said Tara.

They went in the village to ask some questions. As they went further into the village they saw creatures that had a similar body to humans but they were much taller. They had sharp claws and they all had long hair. They were blue and purple colored and had eyes like horses. One of the creatures went up to them and started talking in a different language. The creatures pointed arrows at them and pushed them and made them walk. They brought them to a large structure that looked like a castle. "I wonder where they're taking us," said Tara to her father.

They stopped walking and Tara and her father saw two of the creatures sitting on a throne. "These must be their leaders," said Tara's father.

The creatures started to talk to them but they still couldn't understand them. After talking for a while they started to take them to a room. There they saw David. He was sitting on a small bed and nothing bad had happened to him. "David you're ok," said Tara. She ran to him and gave him a hug.

"The creatures at first pointed sharp arrows at me but then they gave me a room and I don't know why," said David. "They gave me water and food too," continued David.

The creatures pointed outside of the room and walked out. "I think they want us to follow them," said Tara's father. They went to see where the creatures were going. Tara, David and their father followed the creatures and took them to the place where they had fallen through. But there wasn't a portal there. "Just wait, I think the portal will open again," said their father.

The creatures began to show them drawings. It was drawings of people and the creatures. The creatures made Tara, David and their father understand that the portal only opens after a very long time for three short intervals. Once it has opened three times it closes completely again until a long time has passed. Some humans had once attacked the creatures and destroyed their city. People keep coming through the portals but they didn't know who they could trust. So every time they had to take precaution. The king and queen would talk and get to know the humans that come through the portal to assess whether they are friendly or hostile. Everything made sense to Tara, David and their father now. "That's why they first brought us to their leaders before taking us to David," said Tara.

"If the portal opens three times then it is going to open one more time and we have to go in quickly," said David.

"Yes we will," replied their father.

They waited patiently with the creatures for the portal to open again. After a little while the portal opened again and when they got home they decided to find out a way to keep the portal open and talked about becoming friends with the creatures. They got home and the mother ran and gave them all a hug. "What happened?" asked the mother.

"We have so much to tell you," said Tara. Tara, David and their father told the mother about everything that had happened.

7
Stranded in the Snow

Stranded in the Snow

Mia and Layla were business partners and twin sisters. One day while working Mia said to Layla, "You know, we could use a vacation". They went on the internet looking for places they could go. They found many places like beaches with giant waves. But Mia and Layla liked the snow more than going to the beach. They found a cabin they could stay in which was on a mountain called Grays Peak. "Let's go there for our vacation," said Mia.

"It looks pretty cold, do you think we have the right gear?" asked Layla.

"Don't worry about it we have lots of warm clothes," replied Mia.

"Ok then," said Layla.

They packed their things and booked a flight to the cabin. The next day they went to the airport and boarded the airplane. There were about thirty-five people on board the plane. While flying, something hit the plane. One of the wings of the plane became damaged. The plane started descending really fast. The pilot couldn't fly it but managed to control it until it landed in the snow on the mountain. All the passengers survived but many of them were badly injured. Layla's leg was broken. "Layla! Oh no you're hurt," said Mia.

"It's not that bad," said Layla.

Everyone was panicking. The pilot said that they had enough food and water to last them for two weeks. The cabins with all their resources were 300 miles away. They didn't have any way of contact because the airplane's radio was damaged and their cellphones got damaged in the crash. They had to walk to the cabins so they could use the phones that were there. Everyone packed everything from the planes and started to walk. Some people refused to go and said that it would be safer at the plane.

"This is going to be a long walk," said Layla.

"Don't worry I'll carry you. At least it will be a good exercise," said Mia.

Mia put Layla in a stretcher that she had made out of spare parts of the airplane and started to carry her towards the cabin. After walking for a whole day everyone decided to eat something. It had become dark and Mia and Layla fell asleep. The passengers set up a campfire to keep themselves warm and so animals would stay away from them.

When Layla and Mia woke up they found themselves surrounded by wolves. Mia and Layla both became frightened. Mia started shooing the wolves away. The wolves nearly bit her hand. Mia screamed and grabbed a stick with fire and pointed it at them. "Good thinking," said Layla while lying on the stretcher.

The wolves eventually started to back away slowly. They also saw that there weren't any people with them. "They must have run away when they saw the wolves," said Mia worryingly.

"That won't stop us from going to the cabins," said Layla.

"But we don't know the way there," replied Mia.

"Yes we do," replied Layla. They saw that the pilot had left one of the maps there.

"This is going to be harder than google maps," said Mia.

Mia and Layla walked as much as they could until they encountered another wolf. They got scared at first but something was different. It was very small in size. It seemed to be a very young wolf. "It must have gotten separated from its mother," said Mia.

"It will find a way back on its own," said Layla.

As they walked, the little wolf started to follow them. The little wolf kept jumping up and down and nearly bit Mia's leg. They tried different ways to make it go away but nothing was working. They decided to rest again. Mia pulled out her backpack to eat something. As soon as Mia pulled out a bit of cooked meat the wolf came close as if it wanted some. "Hey that's my lunch!" shouted Mia. The little wolf looked at Mia with its big adorable eyes and looked hungry. "Fine, here's half of it," said Mia. The little wolf sat down and enjoyed eating the meat.

After they finished eating they started walking again and the little wolf jumped into Mia's backpack. It started to dig through it again looking for meat. "How much meat do you want," said Mia.

It had been one day and Mia and Layla were exhausted. When they were walking, the little wolf jumped off Mia's back and started to run away. "Where is he going?" said Layla. Layla and Mia looked back and saw a huge avalanche coming towards them.

"We have to get away!" yelled Mia. Mia while carrying Layla on a stretcher ran as fast as she could but the stretcher broke. "You have to try and run with me," said Mia to Layla. They had to go a little slower due to Layla's broken leg. Layla slipped and fell onto ice. The ice was starting to break. Layla tried to walk off but that was just making it worse. Mia reached her hand out. "Grab on quick!" shouted Mia.

Mia grabbed Layla's hand and pulled her away from the ice and they started to run again. After a little while they were clear of the avalanche and the two sisters managed to survive. Mia and Layla were breathing heavily. The little wolf came to Mia and Layla to see if they were alright.

They kept on walking and walking. It had been one week and Mia and Layla had finally made it to the cabins. It had food, water and a phone there. They called for help and waited in the cabins for the rescue helicopter to come. The little wolf started to run outside. "Now what's he doing," said Layla. They looked out the window and saw the mother wolf. They saw the little wolf and the mother playing together. The wolves later walked away and went to their home. After one day the rescue helicopter arrived and they flew back home.

"That was a crazy adventure," said Mia.

"Yes it was," replied Layla.

"I don't feel like the snow anymore. Let's go to a nice warm beach," said Mia.

8

The Big Mystery

The Big Mystery

Falcon was a ten year old boy. He was sleeping when his mother opened the door to his room to wake him up. "Falcon you're late for school. Here, I packed your things for you already," said Falcon's mother.

"Thanks Mum," said Falcon.

Falcon left his house and walked to school. When he arrived his teacher didn't seem as upset as usual. She would give him detention if he was late to class but this time she didn't. Falcon was happy because he hated detention. The teacher began the mathematics lesson for the day. She was asking the pupils questions and everyone answered them. When it was lunch time, Falcon went to sit with his friend, Jim, but he saw his friend sitting with other people that he didn't know. "Who are these people Jim?" asked Falcon.

"Who are you?" asked Jim.

"Is this one of your pranks? What are you talking about, I'm your best friend," said Falcon.

"Off course my best friend, come sit down," said Jim in a creepy way.

Jim acted weird during the entire lunch hour. Falcon went to talk to his other friend, Lily, to see if she was acting weird. He saw her sitting on one of the benches in the playground where she always sits. "Lily there is something weird going on," said Falcon.

"I know, Jim didn't know who I was," said Lily.

"What do you think is going on?" asked Falcon.

"I don't know but we need to find out what's going on," replied Lily.

"We can use our detective skills to investigate Mrs. Jackson and Jim," said Falcon.

"Why do we need to investigate our teacher, Mrs. Jackson?" asked Lily.

"Because she also acted weird today and didn't give me detention as usual for being late," said Falcon.

Falcon and Lily started looking at what Jim and Mrs. Jackson were doing. Jim kept whispering something in peoples' ears. They saw the teacher put away her glasses in the desk drawer. "Mrs. Jackson never puts away her glasses," Falcon thought to himself. "She's blind without them."

"This is starting to get really weird," said Lily.

The teacher called them into the classroom to give in their assignments back. Falcon remembered he had made a mistake on the assignment regarding something the teacher had taught. But the teacher had still marked it as being correct. "I was sure I would get this wrong because she had taught us something else," said Falcon.

"Maybe she has an identical twin who is teaching on her behalf," said Lily.

"I don't think that's it," said Falcon.

They next day was a Saturday so they didn't have any school. Falcon's mother took Lily and Falcon to the store to buy new notebooks. They bought a few notebooks and went back home. They wrote down everything that was happening so they could remember every single detail.

When it was Monday again Falcon went to school. When he got there he saw a sign that said: School under construction for the entire month. Lily arrived as well and also saw the sign. The next thing they know while confused standing next to the school, Mrs. Jackson grabbed both of them from behind. She took them both into a classroom and tied them up. They started struggling to get free but they weren't able to untie themselves.

When it was night time Mrs. Jackson took them outside to the school yard. She got out a remote and pressed one of the buttons. All of a sudden a spaceship that was cloaked appeared. She took them inside and put them in pods and closed the pod doors. She left them there and walked away. "This is really freaky," said Lily.

"Don't worry, just give me a little time to untie these ropes," said Falcon.

"Ok, I will also try to untie myself," said Lily.

After a little while they finally managed to untie the ropes and they began figuring out a way to open the pods. They tried hitting them. It took them a while but they smashed a hole big enough for them to fit through and go out. "Now let's find a way out of here," said Lily.

They sneaked around the ship quietly looking for a way out. They found a room but they didn't know what it was. They went inside and saw a slideshow. It was a plan. There were pictures of aliens that were giving a speech on what they were going to do. Judging by the photos in the slideshow Lily and Falcon figured out the aliens wanted to keep replacing people on Earth with themselves. They could shapeshift and make themselves look like humans. Once they succeeded in replacing all the humans, they will no longer need to shapeshift and would have successfully taken over Earth. They had also conquered other planets in this way.

"If that wasn't Jim and Mrs. Jackson then where are they keeping the real ones?" asked Falcon.

"Why would they keep the real ones?" asked Lily.

"I don't know but I'm hoping they have because they tried to keep us as well," said Falcon.

"Maybe they are somewhere in the ship," said Lily.

Falcon and Lily kept on looking around to find the missing people. Then they found the people the aliens had kidnapped in a room that looked like a laboratory. They saw an alien scientist that was about to do experiments on them. It wasn't just Jim and the teacher there; it was the whole school and some others that were not from the school. They were all tied up but unconscious. "We need to stop them," said Falcon to Lily.

Falcon threw one of the pencils he had with him in a direction that would distract the alien scientist to look away to buy them enough time to untie Mrs. Jackson. Falcon and Lily ran inside and untied the ropes. "Wake up Mrs. Jackson, wake up!" said Falcon.

Falcon realized something was wrong though. He saw Lily also tied up. Which meant the Lily he was with wasn't the real Lily. "You're not the real Lily!" said Falcon to the alien pretending to be Lily.

"No I'm not but you have to listen to me. I'm trying to help you and this is the only way," said the alien that was pretending to be Lily.

"Who are you then and why are you trying to help me?" asked Falcon.

"My name is Niana and I don't want to take over your world but have been forced to by my people," said Niana.

"So, you aren't tricking me now," said Falcon.

"No I'm not, I have a plan," said Niana. "The spaceship actually took off from Earth while we were trying to escape from the pods." Niana sounded genuine in what she was claiming so Falcon believed her and listened to her plan. Niana helped Falcon carry the people including the real Lily to the escape pods.

"I set a course for Earth," said Niana.

"Are you coming?" asked Falcon.

"I want to come but I can't because I need to sabotage the ship so it flies back and runs out of energy. It takes a while for us to get back here so Earth could be safe for a while," said Niana. "Humans can then prepare for the next time my people come to Earth."

"Let's just do it quickly now and then we can go back together," said Falcon.

"It's not just that, all of my people on this ship, including me, have this device put on them so that if we leave the ship, the device will stop us," said Niana. "Also, people back on Earth might not be as welcoming as you if I go back with you."

They arrived near Earth and sent everyone back to Earth using the escape pods. The aliens were alerted to the escape pods being released and rushed to the place where the pods were being held. Falcon and Niana had already managed to send everyone back to Earth. Only Falcon was left. Alien guards started coming towards them. They were going to stop Falcon from escaping. "You have to go quick!" shouted Niana.

Niana pushed Falcon into one of the escape pods, closed the door and released the pod to go back to Earth. Falcon explained everything to Mrs. Jackson and the rest of the school when they arrived back on Earth but he couldn't help but wonder, what happened to the alien called Niana who helped him and his friends.

9
Robert's Robots

Robert's Robots

Robert was a teenager. He lived with his twelve year old brother, Leo and his parents. Robert wanted to make an invention for a science fair that was coming up in two months. There was going to be a competition where they present and talk about their invention. He had been preparing for the competition. He had saved up enough money to buy all the equipment and parts he needed for the invention. He got to work on making it.

"Robert, what are you doing?" asked Leo.

"I'm making fighting robots for the science fair," replied Robert.

"That sounds awesome!" said Leo excitingly.

"You can also help me," said Robert.

"Ok," said Leo.

Leo started to help Robert with making the robots. They first started off by doing the programming for the robots so they could code what they wanted the robot to do. Leo didn't know much programming but he watched Robert so he could learn from him. Leo started working on the eyes of the robot because Robert wanted them to glow. Leo used small LED light bulbs for the glowing eyes. "Good idea," said Robert.

"Thanks," said Leo.

It was night time and Robert and Leo were really sleepy. "Leo, you should take a rest from all the hard work you've done," said Robert.

Leo was already asleep. Robert carried Leo to his bed and tucked him in. But Robert had to work day and night if he was going to finish the fighting robots by two months. He finished most of the programming two weeks later so he began making the body and head of the robot. He used the things he had bought earlier to make the body. "So Robert, what cool features will the robots have?" asked Leo.

"I was thinking of adding a feature where it can switch between different kinds of fighting styles," replied Robert.

It had all together been a month and they had finished making one of the robots and they needed another month to make another robot as an opponent. "We can use the same code for the second robot but this time let's make a yellow robot to contrast with the blue one we have already made," said Robert to Leo.

"Can we turn on this robot to test it out?" asked Leo.

"Good idea, press the on button," replied Robert.

The robot turned on and it had the glowing eyes they had added and they were really bright. "Wow, so cool!" shouted Leo.

"We did a good job," said Robert.

"But wait when does it start to fight?" asked Leo.

"It fights if someone or something looks like it's going to hurt it," replied Robert.

Robert went close to it to turn it off. But the robot didn't let him; instead it pushed Robert right across the room. Leo went to see if Robert was ok. "Are you alright?" asked Leo.

Meanwhile, the robot smashed the door open and started to run out. The robot was going to get away. "Oh no, I didn't think this would happen!" shouted Robert.

"That robot is running away really fast," said Leo.

"We have to catch it!" shouted Robert.

They went outside to the car. Robert had just got his driver's license. Robert and Leo jumped into the car and started to drive after the robot. "We have to make sure that robot doesn't cause any damage," said Robert.

The robot stopped for a while and they caught up to it. Robert tried to make a run for it and press the off button but it didn't work. The robot grabbed Robert, spun him around, and threw him down. "That hurt," said Robert.

"The robot is heading to the mall," said Leo.

Robert realized something. The robot was slowing down when it was running. It looked like it was running out of charge. "I have an idea," said Robert.

"What is it?" asked Leo.

"All we have to do is to wait for it to run out of charge because doing all this must take up a lot of its battery power," said Robert.

"We have to keep track of where it's going as well so it doesn't hurt anyone or damage anything," said Leo.

They went into the mall and saw the robot again, it was walking around and everyone was looking at it. "I hope it doesn't hurt anyone," said Robert.

"Um, Robert, What about that kid over there?" asked Leo.

A little boy thought the robot was a large action figurine so he started to run to the robot. The boy's parents were looking in a different direction and didn't see what their son was doing. "Oh no!" said Robert.

Robert quickly ran and picked up the kid and got it away from the robot. The robot nearly kicked the kid. He brought the little boy to his parents. "We will make sure to keep a better eye on him from now on," said the little boy's father.

When Robert looked back the robot was gone. "Where did the robot go?" said Leo.

"I saw it run into the toy section," said the little boy.

Robert and Leo quickly ran into the toy section. They looked around a bit and saw the robot. It was just standing there and it had run out of charge. "Yes! Finally, now let's bring this this thing back home," said Robert.

They carried the robot to the car and drove back home. They reprogrammed it in a way so that it only attacks if it is attacked by its robot opponent only. Robert and Leo even made it so it can protect innocent people who are being attacked by its robot opponent. They made the opponent robot as well.

It had been two months and the robots were ready for the science fair. Robert and Leo got dressed and they prepared to talk about the robots at the science fair. Their parents were coming to watch them. Robert and Leo presented their fighting robots and everyone was interested in them. They talked about how they could be entertaining and how they could protect people if programmed to do so. Robert and Leo won the competition and they were awarded a golden trophy. Their parents were very proud of them. Robert and Leo were also proud of themselves and each other.

10
Susan's New Home

Susan's New Home

Susan was an eight year old girl. She didn't have a home or any parents and was forced to live on the streets alone. One morning Susan was starving and she went looking for something to eat. She was looking for food for hours. She sat down and decided to take a rest. In front of Susan was a grocery store. "There must be some food in there," said Susan. She ran into the grocery store. She walked to the bread section and grabbed some bread and some milk. "This is going to be good," said Susan.

When Susan was about to walk out of the store, one of the workers came up to her. "Excuse me little girl can you pay for that milk and bread, or get your parents to pay for that?" said the woman who worked there.

"Pay?" said Susan worryingly. "I don't have any money."

"What about your parents?" asked the woman.

"I don't have any parents either," said Susan.

"Tell you what, I'll pay for those things for you," said the woman.

"Ok, what's your name?" asked Susan.

"My name is Jay and what about you?" asked Jay.

"My name is Susan."

Jay bought Susan the milk and bread. Susan left the grocery store and started to eat. Susan later fell asleep. Susan was having a nice peaceful sleep before something woke her up. Drips of water fell on her head. Susan opened her eyes slightly and saw that it was raining and there were thunderstorms. She couldn't find anywhere to go to keep dry. She ran around different places until she saw a playground. She went under the slide for cover. Susan was freezing. She didn't have any warm clothes on. The rain started to get worse. Susan saw a woman walking by the playground. It was Jay from the grocery store. Jay saw Susan and went up to her. "Quickly come under my umbrella Susan," said Jay. Susan quickly ran under Jay's umbrella. "You can stay at my house if you want," said Jay. Susan nodded accepting Jay's offer.

They both walked back to Jay's house. Jay's house wasn't that large but it still looked like a cozy place to stay. When they got to Jay's house, Jay gave some warm clothes to Susan to put on. Jay even made her some soup for dinner. While they were eating they started to talk with each other. "Do you live here by yourself?" asked Susan.

"Well, I don't have a family because I grew up in an orphanage and I lost touch with the friends I made at the orphanage," replied Jay.

"It's ok, I will be your friend since I don't have any either," said Susan.

"That's really nice," said Jay.

After eating, Susan wanted to go to bed. Jay took Susan to her spare bedroom. Susan lied down on the bed. "This is such a warm blanket," said Susan.

"Glad you like it," said Jay.

Jay tucked Susan in and also went to sleep in her own room. Susan had such a peaceful sleep. When Susan woke up she heard Jay on the phone. She heard her saying something about rent on the phone. "Don't worry, I'll pay it in two days," said Jay. After she said that the person on the phone hung up. Jay sighed and sat down on the couch.

"What's wrong?" asked Susan.

"It's just that I'm a bit tight on money and if I don't pay my rent in two days, then I'll get evicted," said Jay.

"Oh no!" shouted Susan.

"I'm not getting paid enough at work to pay the rent," said Jay.

"Can I help with getting some money?" asked Susan.

"No, don't worry I'll find a way to get the money," said Jay.

Jay later got dressed and went to work. The grocery store wasn't that far from Jay's house so Susan stayed home. Susan was a bit worried. She wanted to help Jay get the money so that Jay wouldn't end up homeless. While Jay was at work, Susan decided to go out and find some old cans she could sell. She found a few but by the end of the day she only earned ten dollars. She tried selling other things she found in garbage bins but no one wanted them. Susan started looking for small coins. She managed to find a 50 cent coin. "I don't think this will be enough," said Susan.

When Jay got back home she sat Susan down to talk about their situation. "We're one hundred dollars short and the total amount I need to pay is 840 dollars," said Jay.

"We also need one hundred for food and other things."

"Then what do we do?" asked Susan.

"You should get some rest," said Jay.

Susan went to bed but was still worried. The next day Susan woke up and saw Jay happy. She had put on sports clothes. Susan was confused about what Jay was so happy about and why she had put on sports clothes. "Susan get dressed, I know how I can pay that rent by tomorrow," said Jay.

"Ok," replied Susan inquisitively.

After Susan got dressed, they walked to the playground. "What are we doing here?" asked Susan.

"I figured out that there was a running competition for local women happening in this park and I can enter in this race. Not just that, the winner gets one thousand dollars," said Jay.

"Yes, I know you can win the race," said Susan.

"I better try really hard then," said Jay.

All the competitors stood at the start line. The countdown started. When the alarm rang Jay was the first one to start running. One of the competitors almost caught up to her but Jay didn't let her win. At the end Jay won the race and received the prize money. Jay was going to be able to keep her house and Susan had a new home. Susan gave Jay a big hug. "Thank you Jay for letting me stay with you," said Susan.

"You can call me mum if you want," replied Jay.

"Thanks Mum," said Susan.

"You're very welcome," replied Jay.

"Now, let's go home," said Susan.

www.ingramcontent.com/pod-product-compliance
Ingram Content Group UK Ltd.
Pitfield, Milton Keynes, MK11 3LW, UK
UKHW020422250726
13967UKWH00007B/2767